Pinocchio

Picture Window Books
Minneapolis, Minnesota

First published in the United States in 2010
by Picture Window Books
151 Good Counsel Drive
P.O. Box 669
Mankato, Minnesota 56002
www.picturewindowbooks.com

©2007, Edizioni El S.r.l., Treiste Italy in PINOCCHIO

Printed in the United States of America.

All books published by Picture Window Books
are manufactured with paper containing
at least 10 percent post-consumer waste.

Library of Congress Cataloging-in-Publication Data
Piumini, Roberto.
[Pinocchio. English]
Pinocchio / by Roberto Piumini; illustrated by Lucia Salemi.
p. cm. — (Storybook classics)
ISBN 978-1-4048-5643-1 (library binding)
[1. Fairy tales. 2. Puppets—Fiction.] I. Salemi, Lucia, ill. II. Collodi, Carlo, 1826–1890.
Avventure di Pinocchio. III. Title.
PZ8.P717Pi 2010
[E]—dc22

2009010428

Pinocchio

Retold by Roberto Piumini

Illustrated by Lucia Salemi

The Puppet Boy

Once upon a time, there was an old woodworker named Geppetto. He was very lonely, so he decided to carve a boy out of wood.

"I'll call him Pinocchio," Geppetto said as he worked. "He will look just like a real boy."

Geppetto did such a good job carving Pinocchio that the wooden boy seemed to come to life! His eyes blinked, his mouth smiled, and he could speak.

Geppetto raised his wooden boy as best as he could. One day, Geppetto asked Pinocchio, "Would you like to go to school like other boys?"

"Yes, Father," Pinocchio said. "But I'll need a schoolbook."

So Geppetto sold his jacket and used the money to buy Pinocchio a schoolbook.

The Field of Wishes

On his way to school, Pinocchio passed a puppet theater. Since he was a puppet himself, he was very curious about other puppets. So he sold his book to buy a ticket to a show.

The owner of the puppet theater was an old friend of Geppetto's. After the show, he gave Pinocchio five gold coins to take home to his father.

On his way, Pinocchio met Mr. Cat and Mr. Fox. "Where are you going?" they asked him.

"I'm taking these gold coins to my father," Pinocchio said.

"Did you know that if you put a gold coin in the Field of Wishes, you'll find a golden tree there twenty minutes later?" Mr. Cat asked.

"No," Pinocchio said, believing Mr. Cat.

He decided to go with Mr. Cat and Mr. Fox to the Field of Wishes, and the three of them began their long walk.

The Robbers and the Fairy

The Field of Wishes was far away, so the three had to stop and rest at an inn. That night, Mr. Cat and Mr. Fox disappeared. In the morning, the innkeeper told Pinocchio that his friends would meet him at the Field of Wishes.

As Pinocchio left the inn, two masked animals jumped out and grabbed him. They searched his wooden body for the gold coins. Unable to find the money, they gave up and left Pinocchio hanging by a rope from a tree.

A blue-haired fairy who lived nearby saw him, untied him, and took him to her home. "You poor thing," said the fairy. "How did you get tied to that tree?"

When Pinocchio told her about the two animals who attacked him, she called Geppetto. Then the fairy gave Pinocchio a big hug and sent him home to his father.

Tricky Animals

As Pinocchio was heading home, he came across Mr. Cat and Mr. Fox again.

"We've been looking for you, Pinocchio," they said. "Shall we go to the Field of Wishes and bury the coins now?"

Pinocchio agreed, and they set off together. When they reached a field, they dug a hole. Pinocchio buried the coins. Mr. Cat told him to come back in twenty minutes when the golden tree would be fully grown.

When Pinocchio returned, the hole had been dug up and the coins were gone. Two masks were laying on the ground next to the hole.

"Those two tricked me!" said Pinocchio. "They were the ones who tried to rob me earlier too."

Pinocchio went to the fairy's house to ask for her help, but she wasn't home. He was so sad that he began to cry, but no tears came.

The Puppet Boy's Wish

A pigeon came along and asked, "Are you Pinocchio?"

"I am," Pinocchio said, sniffling.

"Your father is looking for you! I saw him by the beach. Come with me!" said the pigeon.

Pinocchio jumped on the pigeon's back, and they flew to the beach. When they arrived, a sea turtle told them that Geppetto had been swallowed by a shark. Pinocchio cried and cried, but still no tears came.

Now on his own, Pinocchio waited patiently by the fairy's house. When she returned home, Pinocchio told her, "My father was swallowed by a shark. I cried and cried, but I felt no tears."

"You are made of wood," said the fairy. "You cannot cry."

Pinocchio pleaded with the fairy. "I'm tired of being a puppet! I want to be a real boy. Can you help me?"

The Fairy's Warning

"If you work hard in life and do well in school, then one day you'll become a real boy," the fairy said. "Meanwhile, you may stay with me. But be warned, Pinocchio. Boys who play but never work will turn into donkeys."

Pinocchio worked very hard for many months. Finally, the fairy said, "Work hard for one more day, and tomorrow you'll turn into a real boy! Invite your friends to celebrate."

Pinocchio was thrilled. He rushed to invite his friend Lampwick to his party.

"I can't come," Lampwick said. "I'm going to the Land of Play. Come along! We'll have lots of fun."

At first, Pinocchio didn't want to go. He wanted to work hard for one last day so he could become a real boy like the fairy promised. But then a carriage full of children came by.

"Come with us, Pinocchio!" the kids shouted.

The Land of Play

Pinocchio couldn't resist. He jumped up onto the carriage, and they left for the Land of Play.

In the Land of Play, there were games, races, laughter, and shouting. Pinocchio and Lampwick played with the other children all day and all night.

A few months later, Pinocchio saw that his ears had grown larger. Soon after, he grew hooves and a tail. The fairy was right. Pinocchio *had* turned into a donkey. His friend Lampwick had turned into a donkey, too.

They cried and cried, but all they could say was "Hee-haw! Hee-haw!"

The Circus Donkey

Now that all the boys had turned into donkeys, the carriage driver took them to the market to sell.

Pinocchio was bought by a circus owner. For many months, he ate straw and learned how to do tricks.

On the day that the circus opened, the stands were full of people. Pinocchio danced, stood up on his rear legs, and jumped through hoops. The crowd cheered!

But as he jumped, he hurt his leg and could not do tricks anymore. Since Pinocchio was no longer worth anything to the circus owner, he was thrown into the sea to drown.

Underwater

Deep underwater, hundreds of little fish were sent by the fairy to eat the donkey's skin off of Pinocchio. After just a few minutes, they had eaten right down to his wooden bones.

Pinocchio was once again a puppet, and he began to swim to the surface. Suddenly, an enormous shark leaped out from the waves and gobbled him up in a single gulp.

Pinocchio found himself inside a dark place. He cried and shouted, but no one answered. Then he saw a light in the distance. He walked toward it.

In the Belly of a Shark

As Pinocchio neared the light, he saw Geppetto, who had been swallowed by the shark two years before. He had survived on the ship's supplies and the fish that the great shark had swallowed.

The two hugged each other for a very long time. Then, Pinocchio told Geppetto what had happened to him since he left home for his first day of school so long ago. Afterward, they walked up to the huge shark's mouth and dived into the sea.

Geppetto and Pinocchio swam until they could swim no more. Exhausted, they floated aimlessly in the sea. Geppetto began to lose hope of ever returning home again. Pinocchio grabbed his father by the collar and paddled his little wooden legs as hard as he could.

A Real Boy

Finally, Pinocchio pulled his weary father onto the shore. He had saved Geppetto's life. When Geppetto regained his strength, they returned home.

From that day on, Pinocchio never got into trouble again. He worked hard, helped his loved ones, and almost never played too much.

One morning, as he looked at himself in the mirror, he saw that he had turned into a real boy! His old, wooden body sat lifeless on the chair like a puppet, but he was jumping and crying and hugging Geppetto. Real and happy tears streamed down Pinocchio's face.

The fairy had kept her promise.

FAIRY TALE
Follow-Up

1. Pinocchio had a hard time following the rules. Can you name some of the mistakes he made?

2. Did you think that Pinocchio should trust Mr. Cat and Mr. Fox when they told him about the Field of Dreams? Why or why not?

3. What lessons did Pinocchio learn in the story?

4. What is your favorite part of the story?

Glossary

disappeared (diss-uh-PEERD)—went out of sight

enormous (i-NOR-muhss)—extremely large

gobbled (GOB-uhld)—ate very quickly and greedily

laughter (LAF-tur)—the sound made when laughing at something funny or enjoyable

patiently (PAY-shuhnt-lee)—if you wait patiently, you wait without getting upset or angry

WRITE YOUR OWN
Fairy Tale

Fairy tales have been told for hundreds of years. Most fairy tales share certain elements, or pieces. Once you learn about these elements, you can try writing your own fairy tales.

Element 1: The Characters

Characters are the people, animals, or other creatures in the story. They can be good or evil, silly or serious. *Pinocchio* has many characters because the boy-puppet has many adventures. Pinocchio, Geppetto, and the fairy show up the most often. Can you name some of the other characters?

Element 2: The Setting

The setting tells us *when* and *where* a story takes place. The *when* of the story could be a hundred years ago or a hundred years in the future. There may be more than one *where* to a story. You could go from a house to a school to a park. In *Pinocchio*, the story says it happened "once upon a time" — probably many years ago. The *where* of the setting changes often. It moves from Geppetto's home to the theater to the inn and so on. Can you name all of the settings in the book?

Element 3: The Plot

Think about what happens in the story. You are thinking about the plot, or the action of the story. In fairy tales, the action begins nearly right away. In *Pinocchio*, the plot begins on the first page when Geppetto carves his puppet. He says, "I'll call him Pinocchio. He will look just like a real boy." And the story takes off from there!

Element 4: Magic

Did you know that all fairy tales have an element of magic? The magic is what makes a fairy tale different from other stories. Often, the magic comes in the form of a character that doesn't exist in real life, such as a giant or a scary witch. In *Pinocchio*, the talking animals and the walking, talking puppet, himself, supply plenty of magic.

Element 5: A Happy Ending

Years ago, fairy tales ended on a sad note, but today, most fairy tales have a happy ending. Readers like knowing that the hero of the story has beaten the villain. Did *Pinocchio* have a happy ending? Of course! Pinocchio and Geppetto finally made it home. And best of all, Pinocchio discovered that he has at last turned into a real boy.

Now that you know the basic elements of a fairy tale, try writing your own! Create characters, both good and bad. Decide when and where their story will take place to give them a setting. Now put them into action during the plot of the story. Don't forget that you need some magic! And finally, give the hero of your story a happy ending.

ABOUT THE
Author

Roberto Piumini lives and works in Italy. He has worked with children as both a teacher and a theater actor/entertainer. He credits these experiences for inspiring the youthful language of his many books. With his crisp and imaginative way of dealing with every kind of subject, he keeps charming his young readers. His award-winning books, for both children and adults, have been translated into many languages.

ABOUT THE
Illustrator

Lucia Salemi was born in Bologna, Italy, in 1968. Her father, Michele Salemi, is a successful painter. Lucia followed her father's artistic footsteps and began illustrating children's books nearly a decade ago. She lives near Bologna with her husband and daughter, Benedetta.

More Tales to Treasure

Open a Storybook Classic and experience the world of traditional fairy tales told through simple prose and splendid artwork. These safe and inventive picture books feature beautiful and whimsical illustrations that will charm young and old alike.